MAKING FRIENDS

WITH A

FRIENDLY

MOON

Doris Fulton

Friends Forever!

FRIENDS

Sometimes, making friends is easy.

Sometimes, making friends is

not so easy.

Sometimes, you may find that

others don't want

to be your friend.

Don't be sad.

This happens to everybody

at some time.

It doesn't mean that those

who do not want to

be your friend are not nice people.

It is just the way things

happen in this world.

You should not want

to be everyone's friend.

Friends are very special.

If everyone in the world

were your friend, no one would be

special to anyone else.

Isn't it a *funny* thing

to think that it is a <u>GOOD</u> thing

that *not* everyone is your friend?

Yes, it *is* funny to think that!

It *is* funny in a <u>GOOD</u> way!

Yes, it is one of those *wonderful*

ways things

happen in our world.

Not all friends have to be

your same age or color or size.

Some friends can be bigger

than you...or smaller.

Size, shape or color

really do not matter.

A good friend is someone

you can talk to and have fun with...

someone you can trust.

You will read in the pages

to come that Bear, Rabbit,

and Squirrel became very good

friends.

They certainly are not

the same size, shape, or color!

They each eat different foods,

and have their homes in odd places.

Some rabbits live above

the ground and some rabbits make

their homes in burrows or holes

under the ground where

they are protected.

Now Bear, he tries to find a

place in the forest to sleep, like maybe

behind a big log,

or inside a cave if he can fit in it!

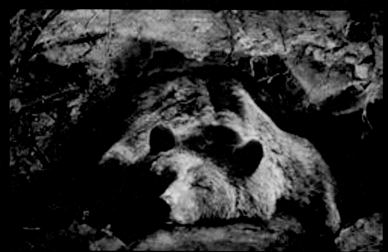

When Bear gets *really* tired

he may just fall asleep on a big log.

Squirrel...well, he lives very

high up in the forest

trees where he feels sheltered and

other larger animals cannot

get to him.

So you see, these three friends

are all different in so many ways and

yet they love being

around each other!   They laugh and

play and are so glad the Moon

brought them together!

****

These three friends met for the

first time on a hilltop in

the forest. The Moon

was shining so brightly.

On this particular night, Bear,

Rabbit, and Squirrel were

out walking, each one alone,

searching for their dinner.

The Moon was shining so

bright that Bear almost *glowed*

wearing his golden vest and

matching hat! Oh, how Bear

loved his hat! As Rabbit made her

way up the hilltop, she saw

Bear and Bear saw Rabbit.

Rabbit did *not* run.

She stopped and looked *UP* at

Bear and Bear looked *down* at

Rabbit...

and Bear said, "Hello" in a

very deep bear-like voice.

Bear's voice was *not* scary!

They began talking to each other

and Rabbit really enjoyed Bear's

company...and Bear enjoyed being

with Rabbit even though Rabbit was

much smaller.

They had such fun together.

Bear decided Rabbit needed a

name so he called her

Wiggles because

she was always wiggling her nose!

Wiggles asked Bear what his name

was, and he said, "Just call me

Mr. Bear!"

So Mr. Bear and Wiggles

were both excited to be

friends. Mr. Bear told Wiggles

he did not have many friends

because he was so big and most

of the time he scared

the smaller animals away!

Wiggles was so happy to have

Mr. Bear as a friend. He was a

big bear, but *not a* scary bear.

They both decided to talk a bit

more while standing there on the

hilltop in the moonlight.

But then Wiggles saw two bright eyes

shining in the limbs of a nearby tree.

Oh! Something was watching them!

Mr. Bear knew Wiggles was afraid, so

he said, "Don't be afraid, Wiggles. I

have seen those eyes before."

And then Mr. Bear spoke to the eyes

in the tree. "Come and join us.

We are making friends with

ourselves, and with the Moon.

You are welcome!"

It wasn't long before they both saw

a little *something* coming up the hill.

When that little something

moved up on to the hilltop

and into the moonlight,

Mr. Bear and Wiggles saw

that the little something was

a little

Squirrel!

Squirrel was even smaller than

Wiggles and *much* smaller than

Mr. Bear.

Squirrel whispered a word or two

to Wiggles and then Wiggles

introduced Squirrel to Mr. Bear.

Squirrel did not have a name,

so Wiggles said "Why don't we call

you *Nutkin* because you eat

nuts and acorns?"

The three

agreed and they laughed

about their new names.

So, you see, sizes and shapes do not

matter when it comes to friends....

And if it was not for the Moon

shining so brightly, maybe

Mr. Bear, Wiggles, and Nutkin

would not have met . . . *ever*.

Over time they became the best of

friends. Sometimes in the

dark of night, they would go back up

to the top of that hill where they

first met and would look up at the

Moon and stars. They knew very little

about their new friend, the Moon.

The Moon never once talked to them.

The Moon didn't have to talk.

The Moon shined down on Mr.

Bear, Wiggles, and Nutkin –

and that was good enough.

The Moon's light made them feel safe!

****

Mr. Bear, Wiggles, and Nutkin did not

know that the far-away Moon is a

lot like Earth in some ways.

Like the Earth, the Moon has tall

mountains and small hills, and

valleys, and even *seas*.

Ah, but the Moon is also very

different from Earth.

The Moon's seas are not made of

water. The Moon's seas are made of

large and small pools of hardened lava.

We have all seen scary pictures of

hot flaming lava spewing out of

erupting volcanoes. Lava looks like

liquid fire, but it is really melted rock!

Well, at one time,

the Moon was almost covered in

flowing melted rock.

But that *lava* cooled down and

hardened into what scientists call

seas.

One sea on the Moon is called the Sea of
Tranquility.

That is where astronaut

Neil Armstrong

first set foot upon the Moon way back

in 1969.

How strange it is to think that only a

few human beings have walked on the

Moon.

And no bears or rabbits or squirrels

have *ever* walked on the Moon.

At least, we don't *think* they have.

What do *you* think?

Wiggles thinks Mr. Bear is so tall he

could touch the Moon if he wanted to.

Mr. Bear always says he doesn't want

to, and then he smiles.

What do you think?

They love the time they spend together. Sometimes while they were together on that hilltop it would be so quiet and peaceful, and they would not say a word.... They would just stare up at the beautiful sky! There are so many stars. They tried to count them once but decided there are just too many!

One thing for sure, they agreed that
they did not have any trouble finding
the Moon!

Even though they are different,

they are all alike in one way:

They all live in the forest!

Isn't it wonderful how the Moon

lights up the forest!

The light of the

Moon shines so bright!

Have you

thought that if there were no Moon to

shine at night the forest might be

dark and scary?

But the Moon's light is

beautiful shining

through the trees.

They really love the Moon. The

stars seem almost too far away

and too many to have as close friends.

It would take forever just to learn

their names!

One night Wiggles asked, "How did

the Moon get up there?"

Mr. Bear was wiser than Wiggles

and Nutkin, and said,

"Well, I know God made us, so

He must have created the Moon for *us*!

YES! That is *how* it got up there, and

that is *why* it is there."

They all agreed and were happy

to think God made the Moon to

give them light in the darkness.

And so they all just stood there

watching as the Moon got higher

and higher in the starry sky, until it got

so

high that Nutkin lost his balance, fell

over backward, and rolled down the

snowy hill just a bit.

Nutkin wasn't hurt. The snow was soft

like white feathers. So Mr. Bear and

Wiggles laughed at Nutkin for taking a

funny tumble. And Nutkin laughed

at himself for tumbling funny!

Oh what a wonderful night that was!

Three close friends having a wonderful

time on a snowy hilltop in the forest,

and another friend far away and high

above shining a friendly light

on them.

Oh, Look!
Someone must be looking at the Moon through a *telescope* so they can get a closer look!
What do you think?

Through a telescope we can see

mountains on the Moon, and dark

round holes that are called "craters."

So one can see the Moon up close,

and still be far, far away,

and *safe* on Earth.

The Moon has no air!

Mr. Bear, Wiggles, and Nutkin do not

have a spacesuit, so they decided they

would like to be far-away friends of

the Moon.

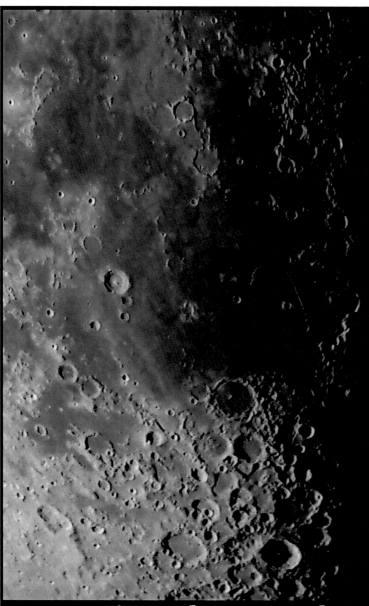

Since the Moon has no air that

means it has no wind...

and if there is no wind,

Mr. Bear's hat could not blow off!

This is what the Moon looks

like through a telescope!

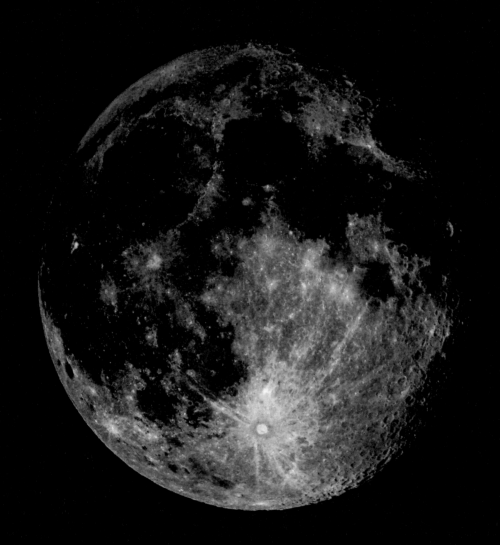

Even though the Moon is very far away, the
telescope makes it appear
much closer.

Along with craters and mountains, this picture of the Moon shows the *seas* of hardened lava.

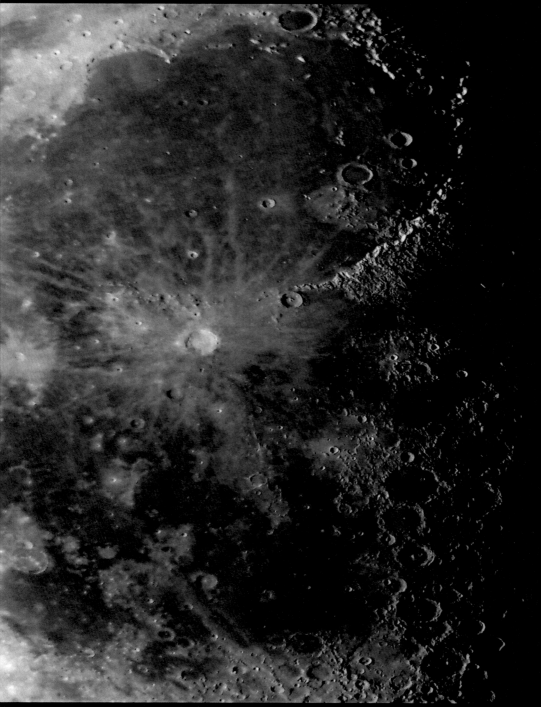

Here is another picture of the Moon taken with a telescope. The *large* crater's name is *Copernicus.*

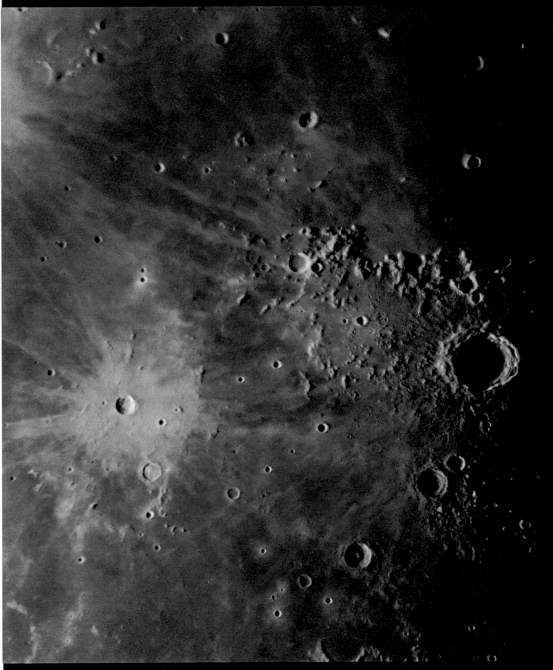

When you look at the Moon through a telescope, you may see all kinds of craters and mountains. They are *VERY* old!

The Bible says God created the Moon on the 4th day of His creation, but God's days and our days are not the same. Our days are 24 hours. When God was creating the Moon He did it in *His* own time...it is not for us to understand.

Afterall, *He* is the Creator.

As you can see,

the Moon is *not* flat!

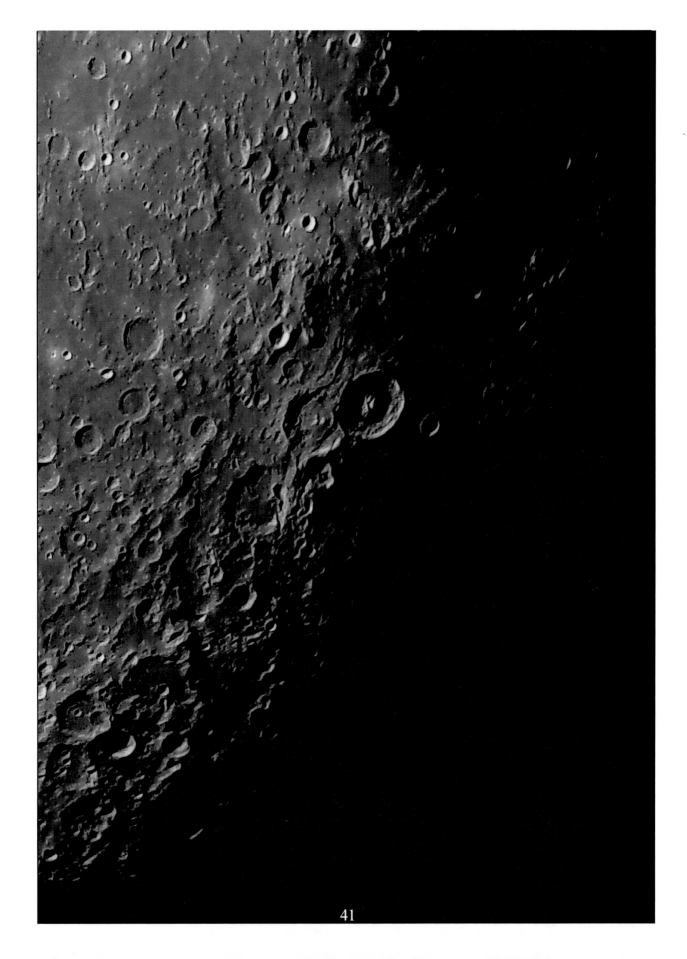

The large half circle you see in this picture of the Moon is also a crater. Its name is *Sinus Iridum* and can only be seen through a telescope.

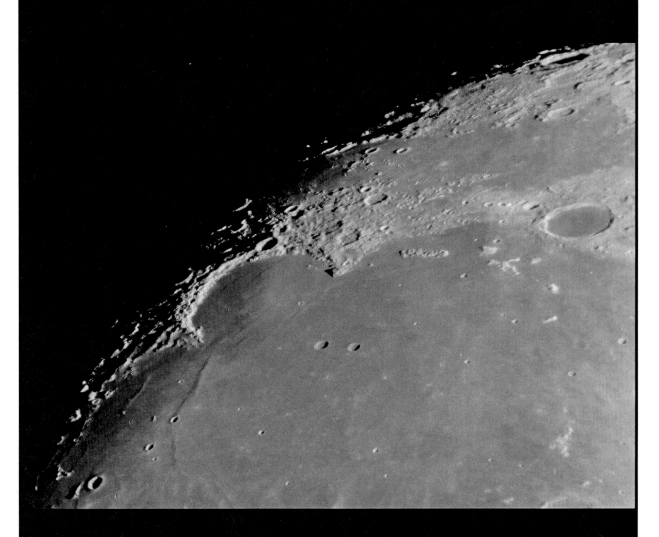

Moon craters are different sizes.

They are usually shaped like circles

with the middle sunken in and the

edges higher.

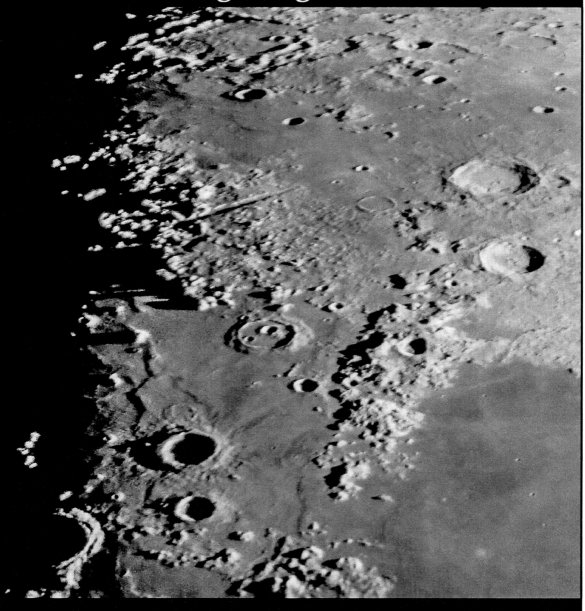

This part of the Moon is called the

Southern Highlands. Look at all those

craters!

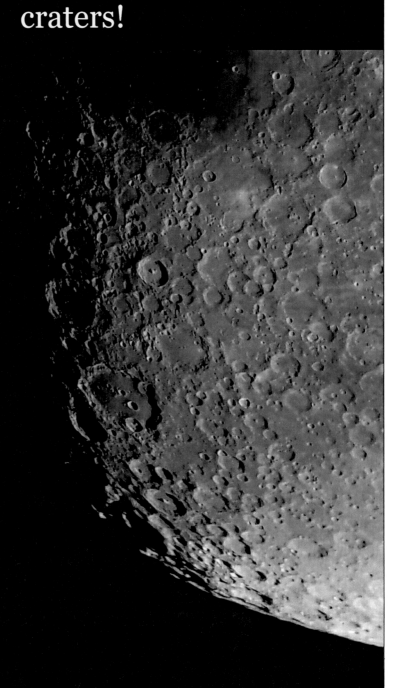

Actually the Moon

does not have its own light.

We see moonlight

because of the Sun!

Isn't it interesting

that if the Sun did not shine on the

Moon, the Moon would be

dark and there would be

no moonlight!

Isn't it wonderful how we can see
inside these craters when we are so far away?

When we observe the Moon over a period of time, it appears to change shapes. These changes in appearance are called *lunar phases*.

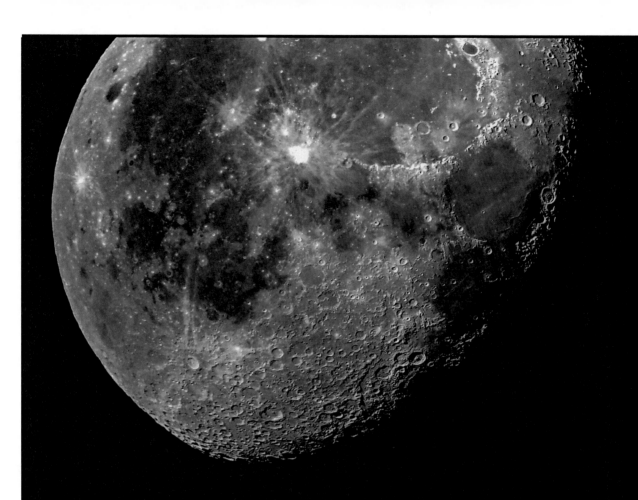

The Moon reminded the three friends

of God's love that shines even

in the darkness.

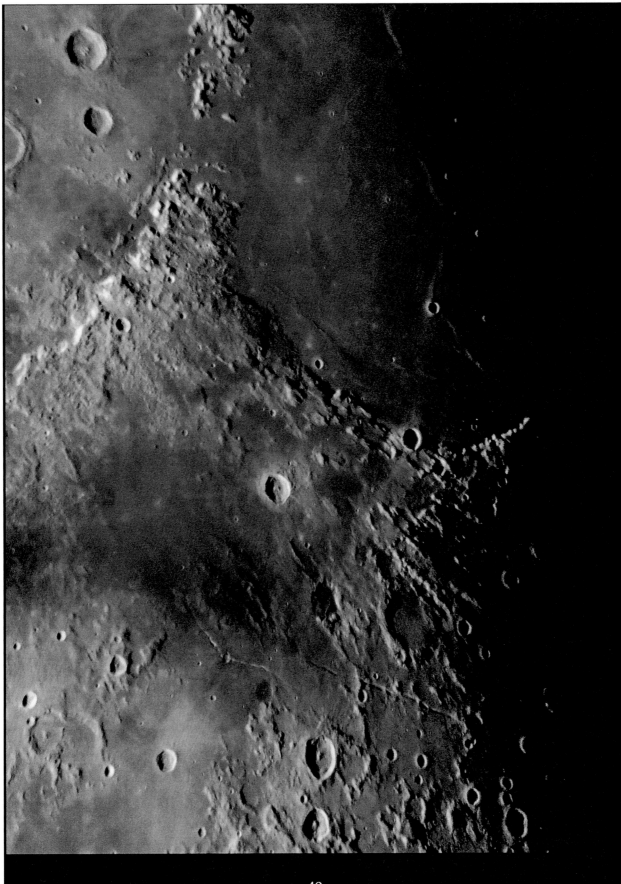

Mr. Bear, Wiggles, and Nutkin said they had *never* had such a fun night! They were so excited Wiggles and Nutkin began skipping and hopping. Mr. Bear could not hop. So with excitement he just stood up on his back legs and waved his arms!

They had learned 🌙

much about their friend the Moon...

even though the Moon was far, far

away. They were so happy to live in

the forest. They had each

other now and felt safe

with the

light of the Moon 🌙

shining through the trees.

Afterall, the light of the

Moon and

God's love

is what brought them all

together.